JUSTIFIED ANGER

How Hatred and Bigotry Triggers Trauma in Black Americans

FELICIA GREEN AND CHRISTOPHER T. WILLIAMS

TABLE OF CONTENTS

INTRODUCTION

WHAT IS RACISM?

"Defeating racism, tribalism, intolerance,
and all forms of discrimination will liberate us all,
victim and perpetrator alike."
–Ban Ki-moon

The death of an African American, George Floyd, in Minneapolis sparked a series of protests in the USA. The US police murdered him in May 2020, and a few weeks down the line, protests spread across the world as people, both white and black, took it to the streets registering their disgust about how the man had been killed in broad daylight. The policeman that killed him appeared to be enjoying how he took the life of a black man, judging by how he hilariously planted hands in his trousers' pockets while a man was calling out for help underneath him.

To give more meaning to this argument, I would also like to draw another example from a police arrest. Some time back, video footage was released of a white man resisting arrest when some white officers were trying to apprehend him. In the background, we could hear someone shouting that he should not resist or he will be in trouble with the police. But only that this time he was never in trouble, he even got into his car and sped away after throwing a few punches to the police officers. That on its own was evident that what our societies call 'White Privilege' is evident in our communities. If that was a black man resisting arrest like that, and even throwing punches at police officers, there is an over 80% chance of him being shot dead on the spot.

From this alone, the argument that police are murdering black people because of the color of their skin is correct. This is real even for other minority races that white people consider inferior to them. We will reveal more examples that support this fact later in this book when we talk about racist oppressions and murders that have been taking place in the US of today.

As this has been happening, a few companies, big ones for that matter, have come out to 'show' support for black people. It is reported that JPMorgan Chase's chief executive, Jamie Dimon, followed the famed knee protest by taking 'it' early June 2020 at one of his bank's branches. The cameras were there to take note of his actions. Another prominent company executive to come out was Larry Fink, the CEO of BlackRock, a giant global investment fund, as he criticized the widespread racial bias in the US. Other companies such as Starbucks also came out and vowed to be in solidarity with what they called their black partners, customers, and communities.

However, it remains to be seen if all these messages of solidarity are coming from a true source (in their hearts).

In the past, it was noted that these companies have not been behaving 'equal' towards their black customers. JPMorgan is reported to have made it difficult for black people to access mortgage loans. This comes on the back of a 2017 report that said the bank paid $55m towards a justice department lawsuit that accused it of showing discrimination against the minority borrowers. More so, some researchers found out that banks routinely place black mortgage borrowers in a higher risk bracket. As a result, they charge them higher interest rates – much less than white borrowers. More so, the reports say that they deny black people mortgages that white applicants would have received. Starbucks, too, has not been spared by these reports. In the past, the coffee company has been accused of discriminating against black patrons.

The impact of such behaviors (especially with banks and loans) will be shown later on, towards the end of this chapter. We will speak about how much this puts African Americans in a poverty bracket for a very long time. Remember, poverty is one of the things that white people use to undermine black people. They believe that blacks are not equally human as they 'can't' create their own wealth.

A few thousand words into this book, I happened to sit down for a Sunday (virtual) service, and my pastor was on the podium, well, on his couch. You know, COVID-19 has led to many changes in ways that people do things, and I sincerely hope this will come to an end soon. So, yes, I was following our church service online.

Nevertheless, what made me decide to add this lovely Sunday morning experience to this book, let alone in the opening lines, has nothing to do with COVID-19, even though it has led to many people going through inexplicable trauma. But it is about an equally inhuman, extreme disease (allow me to call it that way) that has ravaged nations for decades – racism.

During this Sunday, he decided to speak immensely on racism, calling this opportunity as something that God has turned into a chance to call someone home, even a chance to tell everyone that all lives are equal before him. He said this when referring to several protests that are going on around the world. People are demanding that all people be treated equally.

Being from a white background, he narrated the pain that he felt during the first time that he had to go and interact with black people, back in the 1980s, when he was participating in God's work as a youth. He narrated how he discovered that life was different in the townships where he spent days with what he called 'the black brothers.'

Indeed, so many pains have been observed from back in the day until this day. In the USA, history remembers the likes of Martin Luther King, Jr., and their immense contribution to the struggle of emancipation. It has always been like that. And on this day, the coming in of new civilizations has led to many that practice racism into doing it subtly, and it's not easy to see them doing so, but it can be felt. Here, I am speaking of people in power that brush aside such racial conversations. They totally avoid directly criticizing it; for example, they may choose to call it a mistake when a white police officer kills a black brother when making an arrest. Because of this, the USA has experienced several black killings and brutal attacks in the hands of the police that are supposed to be protecting very life.

Writing this book, I am inspired by the need to see a change in our society. We, admittedly, cannot pretend to enjoy the USA where blacks are being killed by the police when they are merely making an arrest? Images of blacks being attacked by dogs, even when they haven't shown any sign of resistance, are disturbing. And, I want to reveal why white brothers (those guilty of these heinous acts) find comfort in continuing on this path of discrimination.

Having said that, we can only go ahead well if we fully understand what racism means. The dictionary gives three definitions of racism, which are;

- A belief or doctrine that inherent differences among the various human racial groups determine cultural or individual achievement, usually involving the idea that one's own race is superior and has the right to dominate others or that a particular racial group is inferior to the others.
- A policy, system of government, etc., based upon or fostering such a doctrine; discrimination.
- Hatred or intolerance of another race or other races.

I would like to speak more about the above definitions so that everything makes good sense as you will go down this entire book. As such, I decided to name the them in their order, the first one being 1, the second one being 2, and the third, 3.

Definition 1

From this first definition, we see a few meaningful words like 'inherent' and 'determine.' The term inherent in particular is of great importance and will help many people understand how to relate to others, regardless of who they are. The term inherent, to me, speaks volumes about how people just get born and discover that they are of a particular skin color, or are from a certain part of the world. This has nothing to do with that same individual, they are just born that way, and that does not make them someone else that people may idealize in their minds. And, speaking of people's skin colors, the world uses this to describe our races, and we got plenty of them around the globe.

These races are in the form of whites, blacks, Asians. I know people speak about the mixed-race or coloreds, of course, they exist, but in the USA, black is black, and white is white. As such, I would not like to dwell much on these skin colors, but would instead focus on the human being – because that is where life is, and that is where greatness is, no matter how someone may choose to see it. There is just one human race, and that's it.

Well, I move on to the second term that I noticed from definition number 1. This is the word 'determine.' The word came after the previous one (inherent) and posed that people are describing one another according to who they are. Yes, your intrinsic characteristics define you – but they can't explain the spectra of things that you can do in life.

Now, racism comes when a certain grouping of the population gets determined to define the extent of things that one can do based on their skin color. And, because the American society, and others across the world, has been doing this for far too long, we now have police officers having the idea that it is suitable for punishing any black person they suspect to be on the wrong side of the law because they deserve it, or because to err is 'inherent' in them?

This book, therefore, speaks about racism that has been taking place in the USA, mostly coming from the police force.

Definition 2

This speaks about racism coming as a form of legislation. We read more about it in history as it used to take place during colonial days, where white colonizers used to impose themselves on black natives. They made sure that blacks worked mostly manual labor because they did not believe that blacks would be able to think when in management positions. However, in these advanced days, it is impossible to have legislation that openly encourages racism, but some leaders, by remaining quiet and not condemning police brutality against blacks, they endorse this behavior. We have seen this in the USA, and people have been so angry about it, resulting in protests across states. These protests spread across the world, giving birth to citizens of other countries demanding the pulling down of statues that were erected in honor of former colonial masters and masters of the slave trade.

The fact that these statues are still standing until this day is an indictment on the part of leaders of countries where they stand. How can a slave trader still be viewed as a hero when there is so much segregation against blacks going on around?

Definition 3

This definition is what the world is fighting to eradicate in this day. Having said this, it is of great help that I point out to the fact that white people have been coming out as the number one perpetrators of racism because they struggle to live in the same place as black people. This is because they (the ones that practice racism) believe that blacks are inherently dull and amount to nothing but trouble, or do not deserve a good life as them.

History of Racism

The history of racism is included in this book so that people understand why what's happening in our societies today is taking place. It helps many understand why it is hard for some people to admit that all people are created equal in the eyes of God.

Therefore, the history of racism dates back to thousands of years back when western countries would buy slaves from Africa and use them for free in their farms and factories. From this time on, a black man was seen as nothing other than just an individual who cannot think, and doesn't deserve to be treated with equal respect as the white man because they believed that blacks were inferior beings – almost the same as beasts in the veld.

The growth in this slave trade, therefore, led to the growing belief that black people were created to serve the whites. Subsequently, all white institutions, white people, and their children embraced this dangerous belief so much so that even when black communities started to fight back for their rights, no one really listened to them. It had to take years of fighting for the American government to include black people's rights in the constitution.

Here, I give an example that shows just how much being black was a problem. And that by it being a problem, it led to even more issues that make white people think that blacks amount to nothing as they cannot create their own wealth.

So, it happens that a lot of white people don't understand what systematic racism is. They believe blacks are lazy or are unwilling to compete. What they fail to understand is, even if we discard the whole 400 years of slavery, the American system has had black people by the neck even up to now. For example, most of the baby boomers are retiring right now; they are the second generation beneficiaries of Redlining (with loans) and the 1933-59 Federal Housing Administration (FHA) mortgage policies. FHA financed 80 percent of all private home construction nationwide at its peak during WW2. The problem was that the government just guaranteed these loans but they were administered through banks.

These banks (just like what they are doing today) provided loans based on risk models that excluded neighborhoods with a higher probability of default. The neighborhoods tended to be black. You would say this is just business, but the country was coming out of the Great Depression, and the government was providing a necessity given the massive foreclosures which the Home Owners' Loan Corporation (HOLC) had failed to refinance. HOLC was a government-sponsored corporation whose goal was to help struggling families avert foreclosure.

However, it became the biggest perpetrator of racial segregation through its redlining policies. Those policies became the standard used by other banks. So by 1943, 98% of beneficiaries were white, who then had a headstart into suburbs while blacks remained in poor neighborhoods.

Why is this important in this book? It is just a window that shows that blacks cannot be viewed as inherently inferior when they have been denied the right to compete for decades. They keep on being sidelined when it comes to the means of production, yet get judged for the outcomes of such segregation. I say this because most of the hate crimes committed against the black folk are because the white perpetrators believe that blacks are less human than them, just because they are generally poorer than the white folks.

Nevertheless, baby boomers you see today retiring, most in comfort, had opportunities that black contemporaries didn't have. White families financed their kids' education through equity loans, etc., from the same high-value homes they were helped to acquire by FHA.

Therefore, black people were left in low value, inner-city areas, and did not have the luxury nor privilege to force their way out. Big box stores followed capital to the suburbs, and only liquor & corner stores remained with them. No jobs, no opportunity. Black kids who went to college had to accrue lots of debt that made sure that they worked for the better part of their working life, still paying for the college fund when their white counterparts invest in real estate and more.

So, these baby boomers had a huge government-backed head start. They had less debt and more access to finance. As they retire today, they are passing that wealth to their children and grandkids. Most black college students are probably 1st-generation to get there. They are also possibly financing that education through debt, and coming from poor neighborhoods;

they are probably bound to have higher interest rates and more susceptible to predatory lenders. In other words, they are starting at negative $100K while their white counterparts have social nets.

This follows them wherever they go, housing, healthcare, insurance and so forth, they have to pay more. So the system is designed to squeeze the black person while generationally rewarding white folks. A black person has to work five times more than the white person for half the step. It takes us back to our definition number 2 of racism. Indeed, some of it (racism) is institutionalized. I am not saying that there are no poor white people in the USA, but their poverty is mainly because of other circumstances that are outside the fact that there has always been a deliberate effort by white people and the institutions they control to disadvantage black people.

I think about the solutions to all this, and we will look into this later on in this book. We will also take a look at the cases of racism in the USA, something that should open a window into how rampant this 'disease' is in the supposed world's most civilized country.

WHY PRACTICE RACISM?

"As you grow older, you'll see white men cheat black men every day of your life, but let me tell you something and don't you forget it—whenever a white man does that to a black man, no matter who he is, how rich he is, or how fine a family he comes from, that white man is trash"

— Harper Lee, To Kill a Mockingbird

According to the above quote, all the people that practice racism are trash. Even if some people cherish this kind of behavior towards other humans, it will remain as distasteful as it is. And the question, especially after the above assertions, remain: Why do people seem to enjoy this kind of treatment against their black brothers? All these answers will be responded to in this chapter. Some interesting facts will be revealed about how people, in their quest to show superiority, actually tell how vulnerable they are.

Racism is Used as a Means of Oppression

Many habits that people reveal in their day to day lives are, indeed, taught to them when they are still young. This follows, therefore, that elders that are racist grow their children in this belief – that they are superior and must be regarded as above their black brothers in society. In the same vein, I have heard of some extreme cases when white farmers in a particular African country have been accused of feeding black people to lions in their farms. These are the kinds of oppression that the young whites grow up seeing, and they also adopt the same feelings about black people. When they see their elders feeding people of color to lions, they equate them to the same deers that they, from time to time, kill to feed to the same lions.

Once such a mindset is born, what is left out is for its bearer to make sure that the black people around him believe the same. As such, they will find ways to show this superiority over blacks. For this reason, we saw a white police officer arriving late at the alleged crime scene (in the case of George Floyd), and, without taking time to understand the plight of the black brother, he goes straight for his neck and suffocates him to death. In his mind, it was clear that he wanted to reveal the feeling that blacks are inferior and must obey the master (in this case, him being white).

What George did that led to his killing, according to him (the police officer), was the failure to show everyone else around that he was the boss because of the color of his skin. Since he was the boss, George was only supposed to listen and obey him. He obviously failed, according to the officer, and found his neck under his knee to prove to the people that were watching on that he is way too inferior to the white officers. Therefore, he had to be taught a lesson.

These are the kinds of people, even though they exist in smaller numbers, that we have among us. It doesn't matter that they are just but a few across the world, but what is worrying is that every society houses a small pocket of them.

Nevertheless, we are describing racism as a form of oppression. As such, we understand that the human race was declared free of any abuse, or colonialism decades ago. But in the minds of others, they did not want the status quo to change. A black person must always be oppressed. Therefore, they use racism as a way of sustaining this oppression. For example, during the days where white societies were still enjoying exclusive rights to certain areas, some enjoyed it so much so that they never dreamt of the day when all that will be abolished. Even as this has been terminated by law, there are certain areas where black people are still not allowed access. And I believe this is done as a way to oppress blacks with a smile on their faces.

Racism is built around dangerous, or rather misleading, stereotypes and prejudiced views that the white society, in most cases, has grown to believe. These stereotypes begin with the feeling that black people must be oppressed. Imagine a child growing up believing that a black person as almost the same as an animal? If that child is to carry that same belief until he is an adult, it will not be easy to get rid of that.

Oppression speaks about someone that subjects another human being to pain using the power that they have. And, when looking at the racism acts that are going around the USA, we see a society that is growing in the belief that whites have more power than blacks. But who gave them that power when the constitution gives everyone equal rights? Once again, we go back to dangerous stereotypes that people grow up believing in. And, since they believe in these and keep on going unpunished, it brings in the government. The more that perpetrators of racism go unpunished, the more that the government of the day is complicit to these heinous acts.

Racism can be Used as a Means of Achieving Dominance

Just like a bully in school, a racist feels the need to stay in a dominant position, and they pick out a race that has been historically dominated by white people. Why is it so? Well, it is because they believe that the law does not sufficiently protect black people since they are outsiders that are just hanging around in their country. It is a fact that black people came as a result of the slave trade through South America. However, outsiders were the ones that came from other countries at that time, including all other races that are not the natives. But as for the ones that were born in the USA., they are citizens now, all of them, be it black or white. A such, the USA has been known to be the land of many immigrants, including the white people.

However, white people saw themselves as being the same because of the color of their skin, and it was easy to isolate black people and ill-treat them. Resultantly, the black folks have been on the receiving end of many injustices in the history of America. When they erred, they have been severely punished, but when they were the ones on the receiving end of crime, no one represented them. When they were punished for being on the wrong side of the law, those who hurt them while, too, being on the side of the law walked free.

One way of achieving dominance is to deny knowledge. We spoke about exclusive rights that white people used to enjoy back in the day. Well, some of those rights meant that they were the first to access education, and on this day, it is easy for them to access capital to venture into as many business ventures they so wish. So, if blacks can now access education the same way the whites used to do, whites have devised a new way of shutting them out, which is to restrict black people's access to capital and capital resources like land.

Once they are kept out, it is easy to dominate. As such, blacks now find themselves being dominated out in the streets, in the malls, in prison, in their homes, and this has been done through how they are shown that the police can harm them anytime and cause death. The lack of convictions on many of these perpetrators speaks volumes about how this dominance is being institutionalized. Having been dominated in the streets, the white society made sure that they are also dominated anywhere else. In the introduction, we revealed how banks have been making sure that not many black people get their hands on capital to start building their own empires.

Racism can be Used by People with Low Self-Esteem to Feel Good about themselves

Sometimes, the reasons why people behave in racist manners are psychological. Many people struggle to make it in life, and they may be white. As they live together with other whites in the community, they realize that they are the least in a group, but in them, they feel like they need to dominate. With nowhere else to show this, they pick out on the black people because they are made to believe that these people are supposed to be inferior to them. And, instead of fighting to get to the same level as their white peers, they become racist and bully black folks in front of everyone so that they feel good about their dominant nature, even if it's not true.

Looking at the above, I believe that some white folks use blacks as mere pieces in a chase game that reveals to people how superior they are. Many who do this are already not equal to the people they interact with. Remember, with racism, perpetrators may feel like they belong to a particular grouping and automatically group themselves away from black folks. But in those groups, some white folks suddenly realize that they are way inferior, perhaps judging with how wealthy they are, to most in the group. So, that appetite to dominate will have nowhere else to be fulfilled than on the black brother. When they do this and go unpunished, they are bound to repeat it, resulting in the indictment of the government for not acting accordingly.

WHAT CAN VICTIMS DO TO END RACISM?

"For it isn't enough to talk about peace.
One must believe in it. And it isn't enough to
believe in it. One must work at it."
– Eleanor Roosevelt

Some time ago, I came across someone, and we got to discuss this racism matter going on around the USA and the world. We spoke to depth about how serious it has become as police officers now believe that they have the right to torture and kill black people as they please. During our discussion, the subject about how to fix this came up, and we look at what both parties can do to fix it, starting with the victims and then perpetrators in the following chapter.

What came it from it was that victims are not responsible for the rise of this problem, but perpetrators are. My friend said that it was the duty of those in government that tolerates racism, as well as that of the police officers caught in broad daylight killing and attacking black people, and others in the minority groups. As such, I raised the questions about how can we ensure racism's total eradication if victims would just sit back and not do anything about it? Should we trust perpetrators enough that they will take responsibility and make sure that everyone is safe around them?

Nevertheless, I believe that there is something that victims too can do to stop the spread of racism across the USA. Racism has broken many spirits and driven many to fear in their little corners (fear of loss of income and life). Many people cannot speak out because they would be fired from their jobs, or if they married a white person, they fear how their in-laws would react if they suddenly scold white people for being racist. Nevertheless, minority groups in the USA must be united and find ways of revealing how bad this is. They must fight/engage perpetrators until something gives. These are just some of the means of dealing with it, but we look at each of the ways that victims of racism may deal with this below.

Make Privileged Individuals know about their Racism

The truth of the matter is that, even though many privileged whites may profess ignorance about racism, and believe that they haven't been like that their whole lives, the fact is they may have been racist in life and never noticed. This is to say that racism may be a result of a deliberate action to harm the minority or could take place in your subconscious when carrying out your everyday activities. Such racists don't see anything wrong with their actions because they live and mingle with the black folks daily. But they sometimes give a job to the undeserving white person instead of the black brother that deserves it more. These, also, are in the brackets of the financial institutions that think it is OK to approve loans for white people and not do the same to the black brother that has a similar risk profile to the white person they just awarded the loan to.

These are the things that happen daily in societies. And, if we are to judge by this, you will notice that many people are racist – the number will be alarming! Such are the people that need to be made alive to the fact that racism is rampant and has condemned many black people into the lifestyle of fighting for a living, which has resulted in them being labeled in a certain way – mostly degrading.

Still on this, the people that grew up in white families that were not too vocal about racism don't see how they become racist, nor do they understand the extent of the damage that racism is putting on the lives of the minority groups in the USA. Just the other day, one white man that grew up in a privileged family confessed just to have learned about racism in school. But he had never witnessed it taking place on the life of a real person. He said that he knew about it from when he studied civil rights, the slave trade, and racism back in school. As something that he just studied in school, it did not even strike him that it was happening in other places as we speak. He had never been to a black community only until he was older.

When he got to these communities, he witnessed how the police would make arrests there. According to him, it is totally different from when they used to come and make an arrest in his own area. He says it would look like someone is just being picked up for a date, whereas in the black communities, he observed that the arrest was like a mini warzone, only that one part will be shooting the gun while the other (black man) would be raising hands in the air.

This is just one example of an individual that understands that he was privileged and was blinded to the realities of the US we live in today. What then about millions of others that grow up this way and refuse to see this reality while they still can? These are the ones I believe must be made to see the light. It's simple how we can do this – to keep on fighting back – making sure that at every level, people are conscientious about racism and how it must be eradicated. If this can be the message in schools, government, universities, and eventually white people's homes, the better.

If this message is driven home, many people's views against blacks will change. I understand that it is hard to change yourself when people had already labeled you in a certain way. This is why, even though black people have gained knowledge in many disciplines and achieved several things in their lives, cannot score top leadership positions in top institutions like Goldman Sachs – where, until now, there has not been a black CEO appointed by the company.

We understand that this is a long road ahead, but the sooner people understand that not all racists are out killing black men in the streets of USA, the better. People should know that while violent racism acts are killing physical bodies, institutionalized racism is out destroying livelihoods and condemning black people to everlasting poverty.

Victims Must Acknowledge that they have Lost Everything

This is not one of those rhetoric statements, but the reality of the day, that by going through all these racist killings, torture, and maiming, black people have lost everything. They have lost the right to speak out and have lost the dignity that a human being deserves.

I believe that it helps to acknowledge that they have lost everything because it is easy to fight a good fight when there is nothing to lose. Therefore, this good fight is easily fought when there is no feeling about something that needs to be protected because whatever there was, the racists have taken it away. Imagine being dragged around by a police dog when kids are watching? It paints a wrong picture, something that will make them not view you, and life the same, ever again. As they lose all the inner peace from seeing such images, you know that gives every reason for black societies to come out in numbers and fight for what is right by them.

Still, on the notion about it being easy to fight the good fight when there is nothing to lose, I am reminded of how white, privileged people ignore some of these racist talks. They do this because they know that by correcting racism, they stand to lose the most. Instead of getting preferential treatment by the police, they will now be treated equally; instead of having certain neighborhoods where they alone could afford (of course via hefty housing loans), they will certainly have to be now content about living with a black neighbor. For these reasons and more, they just brush aside any racist talks that seek to correct the current status quo.

Nevertheless, when I speak about fighting, I do not mean violence and burning down buildings and infrastructure in the streets. But this is done through a show of solidarity as people come out in numbers communicating the same message of tolerance and demanding equal respect as their white brothers.

The loss that people have experienced is not just about the physical pain that they are going through as racists keep on subjecting them through the pain. But this loss goes beyond generations as we see in today's society – where black descendants have had to deal with high college loan debts, failure to access real wealth and so forth. These problems started long back when the white racists denied their black forefathers access to wealth. Therefore, if this problem persists, more generations to come will still arrive in a society where there has been nothing but a legacy of poverty, fear, and pain. These are the things that they would have to inherit.

What brings so much pain is the fact that as they inherit these, their right to equality is completely stolen. They will simply come to a society that is similar to that which was experienced in the slave trade era where all whites were called 'boss' by blacks.

Even little children just grew up knowing that all white people are their bosses, even if they did not work for them. Such ways of thinking fast track the losses that I am speaking about because there is no way that such mindset would lead to the creation of generational wealth, let alone the idea that all people are created equal.

The sooner that people of color, and other minority groups that you will see also experienced immense racism, begin to resist keeping on losing even more of their dignity and means of production, the sooner they fight back with all they have. Remember, resistance is something that is first built in your mind. It always follows an adverse observation that you instantly decide not to abide by. Once the mind is set that it doesn't want to continue in a certain way, it forces the whole body into action.

As such, let the minority understand that they have lost everything and that if the status quo continues unabated, their descendants will come into a world of nothing but a feeling that they are the second class citizens of the US.

Fighting Back Responsibly

I understand that where there is anger, people act in several ways that most do not lead to good outcomes. As such, I take this time to reiterate how important it is to make sure that the objective is always to be put first, then all emotions follow. Many white people grew up practicing racism and benefited from it but still live in denial. They do not recognize that their benefiting from the system, and their continued silence about it contributes to racism.

I can give examples of what we have already spoken about. Firstly, we gave a case about a white man that fought back the police, throwing punches at them and later ran away. This white man, even if he had not had any racist history in the past, he at least knew about the killings of black people in the hands of the police as they pretended to have been attacking a person who was resisting arrest. But there he was resisting arrest in the most violent manner. Why would he do that? This is because inherently, he knew that he was privileged. He knew that he had certain rights that come first before those of black people. Therefore, even if he knew about people that got killed while resisting arrest, he certainly knew that it only applied to the minority – who have lesser rights than him.

You find that the same person can go ahead and show up at a job interview feeling all entitled, and telling himself confidently that I got this – especially when being the only white person interviewing for the job. All these things, they get them from what they grow up seeing. I know for sure that white people working in the same position as black people get paid more money just because of their skin color. This really baffled me, so I asked one of them that always spoke to us freely. He said that they were getting paid more because of their lifestyles. I asked him to explain more, and he told me that white people generally live expensive lifestyles than black people.

That response there really baffled me. This was coming from someone who always claimed to be non-racist, yet he was exactly that by saying that white people have a better taste than black people, and they should just get paid more. There is nothing that can be more racist than this. You cannot go around and putting people in certain brackets and label them whatever you want. It's what I have been speaking about that many white people could be racist in their silence, or in what they have grown to feel as normal.

As such, fighting such a huge battle is not easy. It has to be carried out by sane people who will go to extra lengths just to get the attention of relevant people. There is a saying that says that to kill a snake, you got to strike it by the head. And I agree with this assertion as I say that the snake that is racism in America is very institutionalized, starting with the government. Therefore, the battle must be taken to them so that they bring about legislation that prohibits such tendencies at any level. Secondly, workplaces must be compelled to treat people equally, as all parents spend time here. If they get fixed, they go back home and teach their children about how not to be racist. Fixing the problem this way ensures that we prepare for future generations that are tolerant of each other. After all, all humans are created in the image of God.

WHAT CAN OPPRESSORS DO TO END RACISM?

"No matter how big a nation is, it is no stronger than its weakest people, and as long as you keep a person down, some part of you has to be down there to hold him down, so it means you cannot soar as you might otherwise."

– Marian Anderson

The bad thing about keeping minorities down is that their contribution to the well-being of the country also goes down with it. This is the simple reality that faces all those letting racism stay among us. Here is a good example, if you let racism go on and it shuts out 100 thousand black people out of their real salaries, say you take 5% from them. This, depending on how much all of these earn, or should earn, could amount to millions of dollars in losses to the economy. Besides how much they could have been taxed from that, there is also the money that they would use on their various household expenditure. That money contributes to economic growth – you know, the multiplier effect.

As such, there is no point in encouraging racism in our communities. Now that we have discussed that also white people that are quiet on the subject could be conducting acts of racism in their homes and workplaces, we may as well ask them what they can do to make sure that it stops.

I say this because racism is just like COVID-19 that is completely shifting the way that people live around the world. As such, it must be assumed that everyone sitting at a privileged position has it. From what we have discussed above, it can only be fair to assume that, and the assumptions help bring everyone on the negotiating table, or rather something along the lines of self-introspection. It helps people open up themselves to dialogue about how this can be fixed.

As I have said, everyone must assume that they are racist, so that they are open to taking an opportunity to listen to experts about it. Above all, they will learn the importance and how not to spread racism. We, however, understand that some people may resist sitting around places where such subjects are being openly discussed. But, it surely must get the whole of the USA to that point where everyone is left willing to change their lifestyles to bring an end to it.

"No one is born hating another person
because of the color of his skin, or his background
or his religion. People learn to hate, and if they
can learn to hate, they can be taught to love,
for love comes more naturally to the
human heart than its opposite."
–Nelson Mandela

Affirmative Action

In affirmative action, minorities' rights and past misrepresentations that resulted in their failure to access economic resources and other privileges are taken into account to increase their opportunities in the future. This is done so that the former underprivileged are set at equal standing with the privileged ones. World over, we have heard of these terms a couple of times with the aim of mainly helping black communities create their own wealth.

Why use black people in the above paragraph? This is because they are the ones that mostly went under the slave trade and later on colonialism when mainly Western countries colonized the whole of Africa. Many companies and countries speak of affirmative action but lobby groups, like the Black Lives Matter, feel there is not much that has been done actually to make these plans work. They argue that it is only something that's been spoken of, or, perhaps, written in the form of legislation, yet no one really abides by that. The white supremacist show continues unabated.

Why speak of affirmative action, and why should perpetrators spearhead this? Well, affirmative action aims to balance the playing field between minorities and their white supremacists. But, without the balanced ground, it is easy for the black person, and other minorities, to continue begging their majority supremacists because they are the ones who will be in control of all the means of production. And, as long as their interactions remain like that, the superiority mindset currently shown by white people will continue unabated. But if the balance of wealth is shifted, it will start to change the way people feel about who is the boss, and who is not.

Now, moving to the reason why racists should be the ones leading campaigns for affirmative action. If they are the ones to lead these campaigns, it will be easy for it to be implemented because they are the ones who will now be going for a fair environment, taking it from the negative one that they created themselves. For example, when companies are bidding for projects, or when candidates are looking for jobs. There won't be the need to fear for segregation based on the skin color of applicants. More so, as the privileged class campaigns for equal opportunities, their children get to see what is right and are brought up in an environment where all lives matter.

Respect is something that is instilled in someone's life since when they are young. As long as they grow up seeing their parents respecting, and equally acknowledging the minorities' efforts, they too will grow with those views. All this talk is so that we create a future generation that is free of racism. For those that kept quiet because they have never hit a black person because he is black, this is the opportunity for them to put a dollar where their mouth is. Remember, we said by remaining mum, you are complicit to all these heinous crimes going on against minorities in the USA.

Government Grants for Education

In one of the definitions of racism, we mentioned that governments sometimes have a hand in how the people they lead turn out to be, especially when it comes to matters of racism.

Therefore, they, too, can be part of the solution to these problems by providing grants to educate minorities and get them to the same levels as privileged majorities.

This is more of another action point in the affirmative action plan. Governments can spend money taking disadvantaged societies, especially blacks and other minorities that spent years being shut out of the real means of production, to school. After school, they must follow up with a program that supports small businesses from these same communities. The USA is nicely poised with the SBA – such can be used to provide for small business loans, education, and facilitating contracts that these can deliver on. I say this because the creation of wealth among previously disadvantaged communities is one big step towards the eradication of racism. Remember, we said racism is a result of the fact that some societies think that they are superior to others just because they fall under the majority that controls the means of production. In the end, they find themselves with more dollars from the economy and can easily affect the lives of others by restricting what goes towards them.

An example is just how a racist government may restrict cash flow towards the construction of a new road and bridge in the black communities. Doing so is making sure that any small business that operates from these same communities struggles to get supplies that come by road. This is so as suppliers could be skeptical towards taking their trucks along damaged roads and shaky bridges and other infrastructure. It will cost them more if their vehicles break down. As such, the easiest way out of it is simply to avoid such routes. This way, black businesses, no matter how much potential they have, are destroyed.

Business loans to these societies, as has been mentioned, must be of zero interest. More so, minorities must be allowed housing mortgages at zero interest. I mentioned housing because many banks when awarding loans for other things, they want collateral, and without a property that you own, it's not easy to get a huge business loan.

Lastly, on this part, I would like to believe that the private sector can come in and assist previously disadvantaged communities. I know, many of them write on their websites that they promote equality and therefore hire people on the back of that. To me, that is not true. If such huge companies want to make real change, they should assist small businesses in the minority communities to get Private Equity support. There is just little to no action on that front, and again, the minorities are left only wishing that their brilliant business ideas get a chance to compete with the rest.

Also, the justice system can do more to help. It can make sure that legislation written down about the rights of people is followed. I understand that this legislation already exists, but not many of them are willing to ensure that perpetrators of discrimination are put to book.

Remember that the aim is always to make sure that minorities are treated equally to the whites that control the USA. Therefore, all issues about affirmative action, education, and business are meant to empower the mind of the minority groups so that they find the courage to come out and stand tall like the rest. People that oppress others want to make sure that the oppressed have less knowledge about emancipating himself so that he is kept at that unpopular position for as long as it takes. Therefore, a free mind and a free 'pocket' covers the most ground on the road to the emancipation for the minorities, but oppressors don't like that, and they make sure to keep that avenue locked. Be alive to that fact!

Examples of Racist Occurrences in the History of the USA.

In concluding this chapter, I would like to draw your attention to some of the injustices that have taken place against minorities in the USA. This is besides the already mentioned murder of George

Floyd by the police in broad daylight for what was just a small argument between him and the shop that he had purchased a pack of cigarettes from.

In July 2014, Eric Garner, a black man, was choked to death by the New York police after suspecting him of selling illegal drugs. This sparked protests from blacks in the USA as life was taken based on only suspecting them of selling illicit drugs while a white man can punch police officers, resist arrest, and walk away freely.

In the same year, in August, another black young man, Michael Brown, was gunned down by the police because of a box of cigars. He was shot six times. In all these circumstances, police officers responsible for that were never prosecuted. Fast forward to November 2014, Tamir Rice, a 12-year-old boy, was gunned down by the police because he was waving a toy gun at passers-by, and later on at the police officers.

There have been so many killings of black people by the police, and all of them are for shockingly trivial reasons. In 2016, Philando Castile was also gunned down by the police when trying to reach out for the license of his firearm. Once again, nothing really makes sense except for the common denominator, that these killings are on the minorities, mainly the black people.

If the USA is going to be free of racism, such heartless killings must be brought to an end. For a start, perpetrators must be swiftly dealt with by law, not just to be suspended from the force. It simply is not enough.

WHAT IS THE ROLE OF GOVERNMENT IN ALL THIS?

"It's important for us to also understand that the phrase 'Black Lives Matter' simply refers to the notion that there's a specific vulnerability for African Americans that needs to be addressed. It's not meant to suggest that other lives don't matter. It's to suggest that other folks aren't experiencing this particular vulnerability."

— President Barack Obama

I know that I already touched on some of the things that the government and those in power must do to end racism. The issue goes deeper, and must be addressed from many angles, and I hope to unearth some in this final chapter of the book.

When I was planning on writing this, I remembered seeing something that took place in Africa in 1994. This example resonates well with what is happening now because it all has hate as the drive behind the actions I am writing about. So, it happened that in 1994, nearly a million people in Rwanda were slaughtered by the ethnic Hutu people. They were killing people from a tribe called the Tutsis in one of Africa's most remembered genocides to take place in the nineties.

The deaths were horrible, and from how things looked, it seemed as if the chaos was going to go on for decades to come. Forgiveness was thrown out of the equation as the country, and onlookers perceived what was going to be a new norm in Rwanda – hatred. But, it is the government that took the lead as their current leader, Paul Kagame, was sworn into office later on. He managed to work out a path that led to reconciliation between the two tribes. And until today, Rwanda enjoys a peaceful environment that has led to it being named the jewel of Africa due to many economic projects that the country is carrying out – together.

What did I tell this story? Well, I believe that hate and hate speech can be eliminated if the US leadership takes a leadership role in reducing this. This is so important as they have a broader platform that millions of Americans listen to when they speak. This is besides the fact that they can help come up with legislation that protects the minority. I must say I was impressed by how the administration was swift to come up with the likes of the Paycheck Protection program, the CARES Act, etc., to protect companies from the effects of the COVID-19/

It showed that they could be swift to legislate something if they see that it threatens their interests. But on the issue around racism and hate crimes being committed around the states, the same speed is not being employed.

I must also say I was surprised to hear President Trump mention that the police officer that killed George Floyd had something that snapped in him during the time he committed the act. In fact, it left many in shock because he is the first person that was supposed to come out and condemn the action. The thing with people that commit racism and other hate crimes is that they feel entitled to the USA as they claim to be superior to minority groups. As such, when the president brushes aside such an act, he seems to be saying thumbs up to whoever is feeling entitled, or superior to the black folks.

In the example that I gave with Rwanda, it is the president that leads from the front, and from what I hear, he makes sure that all the people follow on the broader vision of the country, and it is working out so well with them. Problems must be addressed equally, and must not be selectively prioritized, especially when someone is listening on the sidelines to feel if the president justifies his actions. The moment President Trump said that statement, these racists who were waiting on the side took the message all wrong – that is to say, they said he agrees with us. And, as long as someone feels like he is important – or belongs to a certain bracket that the president is in, he will not see other people as the ones that matter to him, especially the minority groups.

The government and its employees must come out in the open and encourage people to speak out about racism as they also do the same. I get worried when I hear reporters comment about voter numbers during elections. You could listen to them say that now they expect the democrats to come back in a particular area because that area is mostly black? And, after such utterances are made, no one in government comes out and condemns that action, nor do republicans then come out later and ask questions as to why they do not win in black communities. The continuation of such utterances or behaviors in our communities speaks of a vast divide that still exists among us. If a black man won't vote for Trump just because of what he represents and not because of his election promises, then our society is dangerously polarized.

Now, to totally eradicate racism, we need to deal with polarization, and the government must provide leading guidance on that front. If the government takes the lead and be consistent for years, eventually, our communities will be free of racism. As I am concluding this book, I am glad that I noticed that President Trump has signed an order that enables police officers to be trained to be non-racial from the time they begin their training. Now, I feel like I cannot write more about this as I believe that the real celebrations must come after observing actual results coming out of it. More so, there is a need to follow this up with real punitive measures for those officers that go on and break these laws, just like what we have noticed in the previous chapters.

Even so, the real problem that we face as a county is that of polarization. People have now placed themselves into specific groups, and it seems there is more that it will take for them to retreat out of those. The problem with hate and racism is that people tend to get fixated on what they want to see their opponents going through –for example, white racists might only be fixated on seeing a black man living in the dirty townships and work only dirty, underpaying jobs as they enjoy the more beautiful things out of this country. When they act like this, they lose the whole picture, and it leads to dangerous actions such as voting for a Republican President not because of his or her good policies, but because of what the generality of the white people say about him or her.

Nevertheless, these issues around racism will draw no proper conclusions until society understands that it must be fought from the government level spreading down to the people. And on the side of the people, perpetrators, and privileged bystanders must start teaching, and more importantly, showing their children that all lives are equal. Doing this consistently for many years will produce the desired results.

JACKART
Some peoples words
were like cheap
glue. They didn't
on for very
A Tale of

LOS ANGELES POLICE

Dior

5 SPORTING GO

Figueroa St
300 S

ONLY
ACAB!

KILL ONE BACK

I CAN'T BREATHE

CLEANERS

MINNEH
Lake
30

35

ABOLISH
POLICE

Hollywood

ACA

25
DRIP
LEGALIZE
BLACK

OND
BAKERY
PED XING

ARKING
942-944
FRANCISCO ST.
FUCK THE POLICE

The Original
FARMERS
PUBLIC
MARKET
GROCERS & TAKE-OUT OPEN.
SHOP LOCAL!
BLACK MATTERS
RIP
TrayTray
09.19.09

LOUIS VUITTON
FUCK
12
LOUIS VUITTON

I CAN'T BREATHE
HOW MANY
BLACK
TRANS LIVES

FUCK
POLICE
HATE
POLICE

Made in the USA
Middletown, DE
08 November 2022

14219455R00044